Blow Me a Kiss, Miss Lilly

by Nancy White Carlstrom

illustrations by Amy Schwartz

Harper & Row, Publishers

In memory of
Miriam Askren
(1893–1988)
"the real Miss Lilly"
riding on the wings
of the morning

Psalm 139

N.W.C.

Blow Me a Kiss, Miss Lilly
Text copyright © 1990 by Nancy White Carlstrom
Illustrations copyright © 1990 by Amy Schwartz
Printed in the U.S.A. All rights reserved.
Typography by Patricia Tobin
10 9 8 7 6 5 4 3 2 1
First Edition

Library of Congress Cataloging-in-Publication Data
Carlstrom, Nancy White.
  Blow me a kiss, Miss Lilly / by Nancy White Carlstrom ;
illustrations by Amy Schwartz.
      p. cm.
  Summary: When her best friend, an old lady named Miss Lilly,
passes away, Sara learns that the memory of a loved one never dies.
ISBN 0-06-021012-5 : $. — ISBN 0-06-021013-3 (lib. bdg.) :
$
  [1. Friendship—Fiction.   2. Old age—Fiction.   3. Death—
Fiction.]   I. Schwartz, Amy, ill.   II. Title.
PZ7.C21684B1 1990   89-34505
[E]—dc20   CIP
                                                          AC

Miss Lilly lived across the street. Her house was little and painted white. "Just right," she said, "for Snug and me." Snug was Miss Lilly's coal-black cat. He was old for a cat, but not nearly as old as Miss Lilly.

I loved to visit Miss Lilly. Her house smelled like lavender and roses, even in the winter. We would sit, warm on the sofa together under the rainbow afghan. Snug, curled up on the arm of a chair, looked as if he had been there forever.

"Just like me," said Miss Lilly. "I've lived in this house for fifty years. My little house knows me and I know my little house. It's my third best friend."

I knew that Snug was second and I was first. When it was time for me to go, Miss Lilly and I blew kisses. It was our special way of saying we would always be friends.

Sometimes Miss Lilly told me stories of when she was a girl. She remembered a lot from long ago, but forgot things like turning off her teakettle or locking the front door at night. She even forgot my name once. I thought she was playing a game at first. I almost cried, but Mama said that happens sometimes when you're very old.

I think Miss Lilly liked being old, except when her hearing aid buzzed or her legs creaked. I remember the day she said, "I had ice cream for breakfast and ice cream for lunch—ate the whole half gallon. Had to!" she explained to Mama. "It wouldn't keep in my freezer."

But she winked at me and said, "You can do that, Sara, when you're my age."

At night, as I was going to bed, I would look out the
window and see the light in Miss Lilly's room. I knew she
was reading her big Bible with the magnifying glass.

"Good night, Miss Lilly," I whispered as I snuggled down
beneath the covers.

In the spring and summer Miss Lilly and I worked in her garden behind the little white house. Snug stretched out of his winter cat sleep and sniffed the tulips and daffodils. Miss Lilly and I picked bluebells and made birthday bouquets.

She knew everyone's birthday in our neighborhood. On your birthday morning, she would come to the door with a bouquet and card, and if you were home, she sang "Happy Birthday," too.

One year on my dad's birthday, she got up early and followed him to the bus stop. There she sang "Happy Birthday" all the way through. The others clapped, Miss Lilly laughed, and my dad was embarrassed.

She even gave a card and flowers to the grumpy man
who lives in the mustard-yellow house on the corner. I told
her I was afraid of him, and she said, "Nonsense! Why, I
remember when he was a boy in knickers, fell out of my
plum tree, and knocked out his two front teeth. That was
the summer he learned to ride a bike." After that I waved to
him when I rode by on my bike.

In early autumn I helped Miss Lilly pick the plums from her tree. Snug watched us as we filled up the baskets with the dark purple fruit. Miss Lilly called him our supervisor. As she boiled the plums in a big pot on her stove, I collected jars of all sizes and shapes from her house and mine. She let me put on the white stickers and line up the jars for the jelly.

But last year when the plums were almost ripe for picking, Miss Lilly got very sick. She called our house early on a Saturday morning, and my dad drove her to the hospital. I made her a card with my best crayons and paper. I drew Snug under the tree in the middle and decorated the edges with purple plums. Inside I wrote:

BLOW ME A KISS, MISS LILLY!

I love you.
From Sara.

On Monday I went to visit Miss Lilly in the hospital. She had my card taped to the wall beside her bed. I know she liked it very much. Miss Lilly looked tired, and we didn't stay long. She told me to take good care of Snug, and as we left, she blew me a big kiss.

After school on Wednesday, Mama told me that Miss Lilly had died. She said that she would not be coming back to her little white house.

I cried, especially at night when I looked for her light and it was dark. It was lonely without her. We had been best friends.

Now it is spring. It doesn't hurt so much to remember.
Snug lives with us. I take good care of him and remind him
of all the things we used to do at the little white house
across the street.

Today we went over to see Miss Lilly's garden. It was quiet, and I walked on tiptoes. But then I saw the flowers! Bluebells everywhere. They made me feel happy. Snug leaped into the air. I danced and sang out, "Blow me a kiss, Miss Lilly!"

And I know she did.